For my best friend Roz – L.B.
For Marion – R.B.

Text copyright © 2003 by Lisa Bruce
Illustrations copyright © 2003 by Rosalind Beardshaw

Published by Bloomsbury, New York and London
Distributed to the trade by Holtzbrinck Publishers

Library of Congress Cataloging-in-Publication Data:
Bruce, Lisa.
Fran's Friend / Lisa Bruce and Rosalind Beardshaw [ill.]. p.cm.
Summary: Fran's dog Fred wants her to play with him and does not understand why she is so busy
working on something special—for him!
ISBN 1-58234-777-8 (alk. paper)
[1. Dogs—Fiction.] I. Beardshaw, Rosalind, ill. II. Title.
PZ7.B8267 Fs 2003
[E]—dc21
2002026221

First U.S. Edition 2003
Printed in Singapore
1 3 5 7 9 0 8 6 4 2

Bloomsbury USA Children's Books
175 Fifth Avenue
New York, New York 1000

Fran's Friend

by Lisa Bruce

illustrated by Rosalind Beardshaw

BLOOMSBURY
CHILDREN'S
BOOKS

It was a warm, sunny day.
Fred wanted to play.

Come on!

But Fran was busy.
"Not now, Fred," she said. "I want to make something."

"I need some paper," said Fran.
"I want to make something special."

Fred found the paper.
"Not the newspaper,
Fred."

Oops!

Fran found some paper and cut a big square shape out of it.
Bits of paper fell onto the floor like snowflakes.

"Not that kind of brush, Fred. I need a paintbrush. I am making something very special."

Fran swirled the water in the jar.

Hey, I'm wet!

Fred was fed up. He looked at the leaves
dancing in the wind.
They could have such fun chasing them.

He took his leash to Fran.

"I can't go out yet," said Fran as she started to paint. "I am making something very special for my best friend."

Your friend?

Fred sat down under the table. He sighed.
Drips of water fell onto his nose. Drops of
red and green paint fell onto his fur.
He didn't care.

Oh, goody!

At last Fran jumped up. She ran to the door.
"Only one thing left to do," she said.

Fred brought his ball but Fran went out.
She left Fred behind.

Fred slunk slowly into his basket.
He hid his head under his paw.

It's not fair.

"Where are you, Fred?" called Fran.
Fred didn't answer.

Fran held out a card.
"Here you are, Fred," she said.
"I made this for you."

To the best friend in the whole wide world x

Thanks, Fran!

"Come on, Fred, let's go out and play."

Woof! Woof!

And they did!